The Ants of 9/11
Last Kiss at the World Trade Center
You can't even imagine

Richard M. Charles

No part of this book may be reproduced or redistributed in any form or by any electronic or mechanical means, including information storage and retrieval systems, without permission in writing from the author or the publishers.

The content of this work is the responsibility of the author and do not necessarily reflect the views of the publisher.

Published by Ibukku.
www.ibukku.com
Graphic Design: Índigo Estudio Gráfico
Copyright © 2019 Richard M. Charles
ISBN Paperback: 978-1-64086-485-6
ISBN eBook: 978-1-64086-486-3

Dedicated to all the victims of 9/11 who, like ants, gave the world an example of silence, peace and concord; and to my mother, Mary Emily, the person who gave me everything... even life.

My sincere thanks to the Ibukku Editorial team of professionals, and especially to Mr. Luis Crowe, Mrs. Diana Patricia González and Mr. Angel Flores, for their dedication and effort.

Whether you believe in God or not, there is one immutable and universal fact that does not need to be demonstrated with numbers or statistics. The morning of 9/11 was the day when the same expression was repeated throughout the world and in everyone's history:

OH, MY GOD!

Richard M. Charles

Honestly, what you are about to read is not exactly a book, despite it having this layout.

My name is Terry, I am a student of biology who wants to share with everyone his views on a type of living being and its reactions.

This text is the result of reading the beginning and the end of the only part of a novel my best friend, a history student, was unable to complete because he was killed in a car accident. His incomplete work, titled *The Beggar of 9-11*, is made up of some moving words which, mixed with my humble and exhaustive work on ants and what happened that fateful morning of September 11th, provoked in my consciousness various theories, such as the unquestionable belief that the closest thing to a human being is the monkey or primate.

Judge for yourselves, although I will tell you right now- there is no greater ocean than the human mind.

In the first place, there is my laborious study on some ant reactions and, subsequently, the only part and introduction of the novel by my best friend, Tom. I'll miss you, wherever you are, thank you buddy.

Double distress is all I notice, I have to defend a project that universally everyone would have believed, but I feel ethically unsettled with myself. I do not know how to tell humanity that it is confused, that it has been mistaken for years and years, and, most devastating, that the human agenda is still determined to keep it going in the future…with the same idea.

In a little over two hours I have to present a project on the similarity of human beings, in recent times less human, with what is commonly known as the ape. I stopped believing in it some time ago, besides, I don't think physical appearance is equal to or approaches them in terms of similarity or meaning.

Nowadays, when someone insults another person of a different color showing signs of racism, they usually imitate a primate. I think that this, besides being inhuman, is not corresponding, because that small animal that goes unnoticed, black, just like the first human beings, is as worthy as the color of any person's skin.

By the way, don't worry, the title of this supposed book deal is a mixture of what my friend Tom told, in an extraordinary way, about 9-11 and my study of ants.

It's a quarter past six in the morning, with shaky movements, I go down the stairs that take me to the kitchen of my coastal house, I observe a couple of pieces of cheese in the shape of towers, similar to miniatures of two

New York skyscrapers, leaning on a handmade plate next to the warm-skinned fridge. There they are again, swarming over those two milky towers with hundreds of holes, like office windows. I turned the light on two minutes ago and they started walking over the cheese with celestial parsimony, each one to their office, I suppose that for them, turning on the light represents dawn, or perhaps the beginning of a long working day. I am intoxicated by their closeness and, at the same time, I manage to perceive a majestic silence. They cross each other as if they were sharing information or letters, I wonder if any of them have to present a report on the similarity of species, like I do. I feel infinite happiness in them, I suppose it is easy when there is an abundance of flavor. I reflect and tell myself, over and over again, if turning on the light means a continuous lightning in their cosmos.

Each one of them forms concentric or eccentric circles, and independent of sex, does its job.

Every time they cross each other, with a gesture, they greet each other cordially like gentlemen, or at least that is the clear impression I have. Information or cards are distributed with absolute agreement. Can there be a love of work among beings? I am tired of hearing that some flatter others because of their work, I think there are other possibilities.

Now, I can see how four of them meet in one of the cheese towers, suddenly there is a split and two march towards the tower that is closer to the edge of the plate while the other two march towards the other tower in the heart of the plate. It is likely that they were talking about the landslide problem. One of the towers, at the edge of the plate, may at any moment suffer a landslide that would bring chaos to the town and, at the same time, damage to those at the bottom or lower floors of the tower. In my opinion, the central tower dominates the municipality, and the tower on the edge must be the border.

I grow tired and decide to go back to bed for a while to sleep a little longer. I will never really know the reaction they have when I turn off the light, I suppose a confusion agreed upon by everyone present. I wonder if the ants have only one God in their lives or if they entrust themselves to my simple tiredness. Will both towers go in unison when the light is turned on or off? Will the central tower give the directions, or will it be the one at the border?

What one does see before turning off the light is a curious scene: a stubby, veteran ant walking straight ahead, met a group of four young men who, in a stately manner, gave way to him. I think it is something that human beings are forgetting, give way... to our elders, the evolutionary chain of respect is being broken, with all that entails. I observe how that group of ants is reunited as if nothing had happened, the meeting was only stopped out of kindness. I am a lover of the interruptions because of this, it fills me with peace when they interrupt me for something beautiful, as, in mentioned case, a greeting. For example, when a pigeon's feather slips through the window and lands on the page you are writing…a beautiful interruption.

I do not have much time left to rest, I am still somewhat tormented thinking about the subject in which I do not believe, but which I have to defend in order to get the best possible grade.

Who is behind what makes me try to justify something I don't believe in? Grounding that question is a task I will have to take upon myself to convince the public of something I don't believe in.

I respect every, from the first to the last, primate of any forest and I respect everything they have given us, but I don't think they are the most similar, in terms of behavior, to human beings; the fact that it is easier to study the behavior of a primate than that of an ant does not make the primate more similar. I close my eyes and hear a tremendous downpour through the window, I think that when it rains primates should be quiet, while human beings desperately look for an umbrella in any shopping mall, or in the case of homeless and beggars, a corner in the street where they can take shelter. Ants also seek shelter under a leaf.

It is very clear to me that in the face of danger, or something that causes unrest, the ape runs to the top of a tree; ants and humans do not do this, but rather we look around. It is as if the primate had a prearranged place prepared in the face of danger, but ants and humans do not. I can't stop thinking about the despair of the ant in the toilet when I went to rinse my teeth, I didn't notice much reaction to the deafening sound of the wasted tap, but I did notice the tremendous increase in speed when the first drops of water started to fall on it. I see the crowd in the street running in all directions, looking hard for a roof to keep their T-shirts from sticking to their bodies with the water. An ant was trying to climb the sink with a cadence or speed multiplied by seven from the time the flood of water reached its domain.

Is the desperation of human beings really the same when they are alone as when they are surrounded by unknown crowds?

It is very likely that a feeling of shared human solidarity is created or that everything becomes an "every man for himself" type of situation. That ant in the toilet had to suffer alone, just like the great geniuses. An earthquake experienced together brings you closer to goodbye and an earthquake experienced alone brings you closer to the beyond. When you live tragedy as part of a community, you approach it in the same way, but when you live it alone, you try to connect your inner self with something unusual in your life, which you probably don't share in your talks or in your daily routine. Ants and humans are those beings that react when, literally, tragedy is upon them, both beings camp out, at times, in a potential incoordination.

As an almost imbecilic student of biology, I feel that I'm wasting my time writing when I'm so young, so don't expect my subject matter to be abundant in pages. In fact, I already feel the fatigue between my fingers and two hemispheres, I should be running through the wonderful paths around my house while enjoying the fresh air, my passion for nature and the interconnection between the environment with my scrupulous and meticulous attitude and behavior. On the one hand, I think it is touching to be so young and face a blank sheet of paper, but on the other hand I feel a huge unease when I see the clock, because I think that there is nothing more unique than contemplating a landscape, that immensity which very few people value.

From time to time, and when I want to remember my grandfather, I hug the trunk of an old tree near my house. Trees not only provide the most important thing, oxygen, but they can become your saviors as they were for my best friend's father, Tom, who told us that years ago, after a tremendous storm and an incredible flood, he was able to save his life by clinging to the trunk of a tree until someone came to rescue him. I am passionate about watching the sun decide to illuminate only the tops of some trees while the green of certain plants await its rays. By the way, needing to cut down and kill part of a tree represents the great setback of my life, because what I love most in this world are trees, but I have to sacrifice them to get the paper to write my little book. I have always believed that dedicating a book is an indiscretion and not doing so is the same thing but with a different target, silence. I suppose I find myself standing in a crossroads and having to decide makes me anxious.

When you read the following, don't think that I have gone mad, I assure you that it is in line with my character and way of seeing life, with a tint, as I said before, of meticulousness. For me, the gum that human beings throw on the ground without any shame will always represent islands to the ants. I have seen ants stop at one of these islands as if they had found gold, not only because of the aroma they give off, which must be a very pleasant fragrance for them, but also because they seem to be a symbol to get away from all the stress that they always find in territories without that fragrance, full of monotony. For an ant, getting on that undulation or gum, represents a "please leave me alone", I want, from here, to contemplate the landscape without anyone bothering me while the wind caresses my face. That is character, with a pair of noses, or rather, antennae, and that is that one arrives at a state where escape is the only possible way. By the way, since I have named the word wind, I don't understand how there are people who prefer to listen to music while they are enjoying the landscape instead of hearing the sound of the wind, I find it incomprehensible and I also think that they carry out the activity in an incomplete way.

An ant's vision is infinitely superior to that of a human being, and I am not referring to visual acuity, but to vital. I mean that an ant has the possibility of seeing an animal being, for example, fly. The human being cannot contemplate it with its equals, cannot observe one of its species flying. Primates can take great jumps, but they will never manage to fly, and they will never be able to observe how one of their species flies. In flight, primates, humans and ants, have decorative wings. It is true that primates can see another animal, different from their species flying, there they surpass us, and, in that case, a monkey does seem like an ant. But weren't we animals? Featherless bipeds, we are not animals, I will not get tired of repeating it. The human being has to be content with seeing a pilot sitting in the cockpit of an airplane. What would the reaction of a human be like if he saw another human flying?

The reaction of an ant when it sees another animal flying is one of absolute indifference. How could we surprise an ant? Are we in a position to say that ants have seen everything just as humans have? They even walk happily over stools, human or animal.

I have heard, like everyone else, about how the human class deals with catastrophes. Have no doubt that it is in catastrophes that humans speak one language, for everyone understands each other with shouts and cries with no linguistic scheme whatsoever, and where extending one arm for another person means much more than a set of letters. Regardless of the country you are in, what language does a dying person speak? Extending your arm as a symbol of help is the most humane gesture there is.

A group of ants had a disastrous day, as a car sped past, inserting its right wheel into one of the puddles contiguous to the sidewalk and causing a tsunami that hit the colony, bringing total chaos to the neighborhood. I see overturned leaves, flooded and overflowing anthill houses, citizens floating and trying to climb as much as they can to the first log they see; more than ever, it is an "every man for himself" situation. I suppose the ants will think it was all a natural disaster, not some despotic wheel and its driver.

Architecture, that beautiful neuron that both creates and destroys. Now I can't stop thinking about the placement of the paving stones in the ancient cities and their unusual geometry, like the water channels that make beautiful rivers for the group of ants, sometimes I see them and sometimes they disappear. Some ants chat along the river, while others come to the bowels on either side to drink. The world has become so viscerally industrialized that those channels no longer exist, the groups of ants have to make do with puddles, lakes to them, which appear in full tar, like bags of stagnant water.

It would be good to destroy some dams and spread the water so that human beings would have to rub their tongue in the tar to be able to drink and put themselves in the shoes of those groups of ants that saw their rivers and canals being taken away from them. Those spaces of water where they so amicably chatted, bathed or simply saw their own reflection in the water. The muddy water of the rivers in the ant society is equivalent to the transparent water in human society. I predict the greatest of all human wars, and it will be none other than the confrontation over the scarcity of water. The lack of consideration that human architecture had for ants will be returned to the bipedal being in a more violent way.

The human being will become perfect the day he looks over there where he steps and leaves his mark.

As a mediocre being, I will never forget when, walking in the moonlight, I stepped on a group of ants that formed an immense path, a troop made up of thousands of them. The silhouette of my shoes produced a real massacre. On that path of almost two meters of ants, with comings and goings as if it were a modern road, close to where it happened, I could see that, in spite of my indiscriminate massacre in the form of a stomping, another group of ants was leading a peaceful life. For them, what had just happened did not exist five feet away. Does any of this reaction ring a bell? I could see an absolute chaos at the site of the impact of my sole, I won't get into details since there were bodies, but I could see gestures of total nervousness and also gestures of infinite solidarity. I can testify that at that moment, I saw how they spoke the same language as humans, in the face of catastrophes. My shoe hit them like a meteorite, but they did not need it to be made of rock; being made of rubber had already done them a lot of damage. And what about the proximity?

I still remember that horrible cold in the winter season last year; when I was going to one of my favorite cafes, I took out my protocol handkerchief from my pocket to blow my nose, there I found an ant. My body was cut up when I saw it trapped in a crumpled piece of paper and I imagined what must have happened in my left pocket in total darkness. Yes, fellows, I'm still curled up with respect.

Can you imagine a policeman, with a rubber truncheon in his hand, asking a well-meaning trucker to stop on his way because there is a column or a stream of ants trying to cross the road? I can imagine that unhinged driver looking at the cop with a crazy look on his face and saying, "You're not wearing a cop's uniform, and you're wearing a nutter's uniform!" The respect you may have for an ant should be inversely proportional to that given to the elderly. I still remember, in one of the stateliest cities in the world, seeing a grandfather and grandson crossing a street with little traffic and witnessing the old man walking at a swinging pace. Today, where respect for the old man is in question, it would be very good to compare the speed of an ant with that of an old man, to understand that respect intrinsically carries a speed, if you pass it, you are simply disturbing it. We do not live in a dynamic society, but in a society that corners the elderly, it should be a priority that children are educated to respect them.

The policeman would have had no choice but to let the vocal driver pass, causing a mass killing of ants. The old man managed to cross the road with wet feet, though, because after waiting the driver accelerated so hard that the splash from the puddle reached the man's nails.

They were just columns of ants whose purpose was to move pipe shells, used as sheds for the lack of an autumn. Let us not forget that, for them, the fallen leaves are a roof and, for us, a brown landscape of melancholy. I come to the sad conclusion that the slowness of an ant is as annoying as the slowness of an old man, the ant was moving shells and the old man was leaning on a stick. No matter what you hold or carry in your hand, you do not comply with the speed imposed on you by society. Neither the ants, nor that old man, nor the "crazy cop", nor I, are fit for this world of revolution.

Which society do you prefer? The one that bets on acceleration, taking and crushing the shells and the insightfulness; or the parsimony of an old man crossing a street with his eyes on the ground while he shows you one of his ears, as if to say: "There's my ear as a target for your insults! Go ahead! Accelerate!"

When the twilight of your life arrives, or you get older, you inevitably slouch, and your gaze unfailingly... turns to the ground. Your proud and dominant gaze runs out, you cling to what is next to your feet; the extreme slowness of your movements leads you to relate it to the cadence of an ant, everything works in a special way.

Once I talk about older people, I can't help but remember Walter, my grandfather a potter, who spent his time modeling clay with his silent gaze and his huge white beard, which every day ended up brown at the bottom. Honestly, I think it was him who transmitted to me the detailed and perfectionist character, the one who made me so analytical and scrupulous with nature and, consequently, with the human being. You can measure a person's respect for another person by the degree of respect they have for nature. It was he, my grandfather, who told me that in order for human beings to arrive at a complete respect between equals, we should first reach a sepulchral look at tiny beings that do not harm anyone - the ants. Funnily enough, my grandfather always told me: "There's only one who can sear the sun" he paused "the human being!" At first I didn't understand anything about his way of seeing respect, but with one of his genuine explanations he left me stunned, he explained me that when he met his classmates in the school yard, long time ago, several of them were dedicated to trampling the ants that walked next to an old tree. He told me that one cannot be a virtuoso when, for example, making buildings or painting a beautiful picture, if one is not a virtuoso with living beings. What an ingenious conclusion he came to, with the passage of time I have reached the feeling that he is absolutely right. We must find the ore and the gold nuggets in human behavior, not in the material sphere.

In another of his teachings, my grandfather once told me, "Don't open your umbrella if it will double-soak the person next to you," because he also had tremendous respect for neighbor and for nature. In another memorable sentence, he said: "If you treat nature well, you can even caress a cactus! I can imagine my grandfather being a little nipper and pushing his schoolmates aside, telling them "Why do you trample on those helpless ants?, there's no other way to entertain yourself at school?", almost a divine or prophetic episode. This episode, told with passion by my grandfather, made me decide on everything that surrounds biology.

I am interested in modeling the character of the human being, as my grandfather did with those classmates or with their pots and precious earthenware vases. I still remember the day when I was able to make one with his help, that little vase, which I contemplate every day when I go to the kitchen to have breakfast, has a special charm, and every day that I pass by it when I get up, I feel as if my grandfather were saying me "good morning, Champ! Good morning, Terry!

One might ask, as I've done, if that extreme look at animals isn't a bit of an exaggeration, that's not the issue here, what about the animals we eat, of course one wants the best food, but I mean those animals that have no contact with humans, those that are tremendously respectful, that never bother us, and instead we give them back their rusty currency or pay them back in terror. I think that's where my grandfather's reaction at school comes from. If I had to sum it up in one sentence or in the form of a prayer, the most correct form would be: "leave alone those who leave us alone!

I have another unforgettable anecdote from my grandfather, applied to the human being. He once told me that a brother of his, named Michael, went to fish at one of the mouths of one of the dirtiest rivers that flowed into the sea every weekend, weather permitting. He had been practicing fishing in that corner of the city for a couple of years. Almost everyone who passed by would stop and ask him "how come you are in this area fishing considering how dirty the river is", Michael, who had an almost infinite patience, would always answer, in a nice way, the same thing: "there are many days in which the reflection of the moon is stamped on the mouth, and I love that". My uncle Michael's answer was a half-truth, because it was true that the moon reflected, it was almost like a mirror wrapped in the sun, but. However, the main reason was that Michael... had not gone to the same place to fish for more than half a century. In other words, that was the spot and hiding place where he fished with his dear father and, for him, this meant it was a special and intimate place. The human mind has a negative predisposition when something doesn't fit its expectations, as soon as it observes that the pieces of the puzzle don't fit according to its vision of the world, everything becomes negative. How does the mouth of a dirty river fit have to do with a man fishing? Will he eat or have the courage to cook what he catches? Will he catch an infection from what he captures? The pejorative thoughts on full display, but there is a more perfect puzzle than the one you have in mind. That man knew perfectly well why he was fishing there. He didn't skip a weekend in the summer to do fishing trips and reminisce about old and beautiful memories of his childhood, without caring if any fish or citizen took the bait. After such a majestic anecdote, I have no choice, as a biologist or candidate, but to get angry with the thoughtless society, society that goes a diabolical speed with his thoughts and does not reflect as my grandfather, a patient craftsman, would. Undoubtedly, I think that introspection is being sacrificed. In the world of education it is necessary to work on predisposition before literacy, because a person can become very cultured, in knowledge, but he can commit terrible acts because, while he has been trained in knowledge, he has not been trained in predisposition towards that knowledge. I will put it another way, I could be stroking the leaves of my favorite pot and not be attentive or know when and how much water it needs or vice versa. We must have the knowledge of what a plant needs and at the same time a gentlemanly and lordly treatment towards the plant; that is the perfect conjunction. It is a question of priorities, the predisposition is not more than a cordial, but transcendental, introduction towards a correct education.

When my grandfather told me how his classmates had fun next to the tree, I think the tree probably also had fun watching them play. I thought that after hurting those poor ants, the next victim would be the tree itself, which was smiling at the time. The sooner the bad predisposition is addressed, the fewer beings will be harmed. Don't forget something very important, predisposition before anything, can make that person, although not educated, carry out the greatest task in the world. The history of the prophets is the history of the challenge to letters, that is, to renounce letters in order to form wonderful words from them.

I will be a little cruel now, my grandfather, who said goodbye to life because of a problem with his prostate, told the family, not me because he only told me nice things, that once, when he had no choice but to urinate anyway, because of his illness, he entered a restaurant to try to urinate and before reaching the service door, as if it were a border post, the owner said "sir, you have to consume in order to use the toilet". My grandfather, who was a man of old manners when we refer to health, immediately thought "I am in a public place and I have the right to take care of my needs and my health". My grandfather was never late for a romantic date or a business meal, he hadn't been in a restaurant in many years, and he was no longer aware of the fact that things revolve around money. No one was to blame, not my grandfather who had a health problem, not the waiter, not the owner who didn't know what the story was about. My grandfather didn't spend much time explaining himself to strangers either, or so I think, judge for yourself. However, this does beg the question, where would you place the two opposing predispositions? My grandfather's predisposition as opposed to the predisposition of the restaurant owner; both of them, in their own way, were craftsmen, one in the kitchen and the other in pottery; the head chef, would place the food on the clay dishes that my grandfather had made, molded and delivered curiously to that same restaurant several years ago. The two, at the time, complemented each other, were victorious and benefited, since my grandfather was working one whole summer to deliver a consignment of four dozen dishes of pure craftsmanship to the restaurant owners. The new restaurant owner did not know where they came from. Time mixes things up and new people appear who do not know past stories; these people in turn form new stories and new dispositions or points of view. In spite of the small displeasure my grandfather took in the entrance of the restaurant, he managed to enter the bathroom and was able to relieve himself. That's how things are, my grandfather showing his vulnerability and at the same time showing magnanimity.

I get up to run away from home in order to face my own maze. I don't think, I insist, that the closest thing to man is a primate, even on a gastronomic level humans and ants eat everything, not to mention the equivalence in attraction to sweet taste. Never be guided by physical appearance, which is my best advice as a future biologist.

I go down the stairs and smash my ring finger against one of the towers of cheese unleashing a tremendous unrest and chaos in the ants that are there, one of the towers collapses while the other suffers an immense tremor. I have crushed one of the ants, and, in a gesture of absolute solidarity to them, I see how one approaches the most affected one to drag it out as well as it can; two other ants move aimlessly, as if they did not know where to go; seconds later, the second impact against the other tower of cheese makes the chaos even worse. I watch the ants fall from the towers to the bottom of the plate. I don't believe in the suicide of ants, in that aspect they show more spiritual strength than humans, they prefer death to impact them than to impact themselves on death. They cling to the walls as much as they can to keep from falling and they bet on holding on, without suspecting that another one of my fingers, as if it were an airplane, might impact again. Despair reigns in both dairy buildings; between them, just as in human beings, the instinct of "every man for himself" is born. I observe how they escape through the back of the plate, fleeing without contemplation. Those who decide to stay, try to sneak through the lower area of both towers to try to rescue those who are among the "rubble". Both reactions are very human, some flee because of fear and the more experienced ones, physically and psychologically, try to help and save lives. Blocks of cheese crush the antennae and legs of some of them, causing tremendous crying and pain. The tears of many of the ants cause the pores contained in both towers of cheese, which, as I said at the beginning, resemble any New York skyscraper, to melt and create landslides.

I see how one of the ants, in the north tower, tries to cling as well as possible to one of the pores that protrude so as not to fall.

The impact of one of my fingers has caused most of its legs to be paralyzed. Both towers are on the ground, the desolation can be felt dramatically. It is the picture of destruction and how one human being can undermine the happiness of a whole troop of ants who were simply doing their job or chatting about their future. Would they do the same to us? I open the piece of bread and take the jam out of the fridge to spread it, so I can have something to eat before I showcase my work. I see my grandfather's vase, that vase that reminds me that what I love and appreciate most in this world is, in the end, the most common things. Before taking the plate with the cheese towers I remember that I cannot do any harm to those poor ants. I take out the plate with the two towers of cheese and take them to a big flowerpot next to the entrance door. They are in their heaven, safe and sound, surrounded by food and nature. Everything was, for them and for me, a dismal nightmare.

The following words correspond to the unfinished work, due to a traffic accident, of my great friend and former university colleague Tom.

I still remember Toby, my dog, who always accompanied me wherever my wheelchair went. He was so affectionate that I could not describe him in his entirety in an objective way. Strong, with a shiny brown coat and always ready to give all his goodness to human beings, especially to the needy like me.

Years after all that happened, and living now in Chicago, the beautiful city that entangles my feelings in its skyscrapers, I cannot erase from my memory what happened. As I sleep, a multitude of images come to my mind in the form of a storm, but there is one that stands out above all others: the body of Mr. Parker, very close to my wheelchair, after having jumped from one of the two twin towers that were knocked down that indescribable morning of September 11, 2001. He was my friend and the person who made it possible for me to be in the city of my dreams today, because he was the one who paid the fare with which I was able to return to the place where I was born. Thanks to him, I was able to wet my hands again in Lake Michigan.

That morning, Mr. Parker left a beautiful Californian woman and their two wonderful daughters; he also left me. I cannot express the sadness I felt when, amidst the tremendous confusion, I could see that it was his face.

He was from Chicago, just like me, and a Chicago Bulls fan.

Almost every morning he would bring me a snack and a juice while he enthusiastically commented on some of the mythical plays of the best player in the history of basketball, Michael Jordan; that brought us together.

My dog, Toby, immediately recognized Mr. Parker, it was the most overwhelming image I had seen in my 45 years of life, Toby licking my friend's face. I have no breath or tears to describe the scene, but I have a total need to share what I experienced. I honestly believe that my pet would never make a difference in reporting love and affection for a person in need of help, that morning Mr. Parker needed it, but you have to believe me when I say that those moments were the most dramatic of my life, and at the same time, the most chilling. I had the feeling that Toby, my dog, was the last one to give a kiss at the World Trade Center. Yes, it was the last kiss. I could raise my head to the sky and see that Mr. Parker was not the only one who jumped into the void, there were numerous people who decided to put an end to the most beautiful gift that humanity offers you: life. Now I am not 45 years old, I have a few more years under my belt, and I can assure you that morning changed the world.

Besides Toby, I was always accompanied by a small transistor and some clothes that covered my battered legs, which one day decided not to take another step. On that morning, just as Toby kissed Mr. Parker's face, or rather, kissed his soul, I would have liked to give a big hug to his wife and his two beautiful young daughters. I had the opportunity to see his family in a picture that he kept as if it were gold in his wallet. Last Christmas I had the opportunity to see them. At the mentioned dawn, I was the first person to see Mr. Parker dead, I was screaming and yelling for help, but my voice was drowning in an aura of sirens and chaos. There was a confusion never before seen in New York City.

People walked around like crazy ants, moving everywhere and nowhere at the same time.

I'll always say the same thing, I've seen many ants on my food and no food was left infected; I still believe that in the tiniest things are the solutions. I remember my teacher asking me, quite rightly, "what are you looking at?" I answered "that ant walking among the tiles as if it were floating on a dry river. Years later, sadness aside, I'm like that ant.

This city is known as the best in the world, it has quality and warmth, it is capable of overcoming all kinds of chaos, but on the morning of the 11th, I think only Toby knew that the tragedy that was coming, surpassed all records of disasters. The ground made the wheels of my chair tremble, the pear and the apple fell from my lap and a huge crash hit my eardrum; from almost a close-up, I could see something crashing into the other tower. A lot of smoke appeared at the top of one of the two towers. My favorite subject in school was always volcanoes and everything related to nature; in those moments, I felt as if a volcano was erupting. I saw Mrs. Conrad pass by, she was running away from the center of the volcano. Mrs. Conrad is a very beautiful woman who that day did not remember to say goodbye to me. She always finished her workday at 3 p.m., but this time she left earlier. She always gave me a smile that made my heartbeat. I daydreamed every day of inviting her to dinner to tell her how beautiful and pleasant she was and to thank her for always saying hello to me. She managed to escape, that morning, from the terrible New York anthill.

I have always believed that the greeting is the most valuable thing a human being has, the first look or the first handshake can make you enter a new dimension, the one where only the best human beings can reach. Mrs. Conrad, possessed by fear, decided not to greet me, then I understood everything, she always had a caress for Toby, although, sometimes, she did not like the effusivity of my dear dog, she felt that it dissolved her hand make-up.

You know something, both towers were made up of wonderful people, not just businesspeople. It was the first time, and only time in my life, that I could see a library in the air, suspended in the sky, I can't count the amount of papers hovering over the sky of New York, I suppose it would reveal a lot of immeasurable financial secrets, but in those moments I realized human beings do not live on papers, but on humanity, and believe me that Mr. Parker and Mrs. Conrad managed important financial portfolios, but who would care in those moments? My eyes saw Mrs. Conrad running like a little girl in search of her home with one goal: to give a hug to her dear mother, whom she adored, something Mr. Parker would never do again.

Sometimes I say to myself "how much it takes for a human being to show his feelings". In those hours I was able to witness the most sincere gestures and the truest tears; it was not like an acid rain, but a constellation of feelings on the surface that made me, for the first time in many years, begin to notice how my legs were shaking; the last time I had had that feeling was when I was a child, when my mother was taking me to Lake Michigan, in Chicago. I consider myself a beggar with medium to high knowledge about what is going on in the world, and what was happening that day was a dislocation of feelings.

I must tell you how Mr. Rasuini, a muslim man from Lebanon, was helping to Mr. Marot, a hebrew man who one daydreamed of New York and decided to stay. The fact is that humans should be like ants in that respect, not having a nationality. A huge number of older people are cared for every day by people of other nationalities, people who kiss the ground when they arrive in lands other than where they were born. Those tiny beings have an advantage over us there, I have always believed that the most perfect society is the one of the ants, besides being the best hierarchical society.

My transistor was the mouth of the Chicago River, where all the news talked about the same thing, chaos in the capital of the world and a lot of people riding the streets without any direction. I decided to get away from the North Tower, which was gushing smoke, I grabbed Toby and made up my mind not to look at Mr. Parker's body lying on the ground, it was shocking to see how my dog was the last to say goodbye to him, as I said before, the last kiss.

If you look at when you go to a friend's house for the first time and run into their dog... the animals, in this case dogs, always say the last goodbye..., in which case, Toby lived up to the prediction.

On the 11th I saw my own feelings right under my nose, without being able to respond or react to them, I felt absolutely overcome by the events I was seeing and I ask God's forgiveness for almost not being able to ask for help for the man who made me find myself in my dream city today. I believe that, in those previous days, in a prophetic way, Mr. Parker gave me the money to forget about New York and all the difficult scenes that I had to live and return to the city where I was born, you decide, I will never know.

There are people who have a lot of money, but at the same time have an enormous solidarity, like Mr. Parker.

The hardest scenes that a person can suffer are those that do not need to open any kind of locks, those that come without a previous greeting or those that wake up without needing breakfast, and that morning all the precepts were aligned. I walked away about twenty-five minutes (don't forget that those of us in wheelchairs don't calculate distance by miles, but by minutes) from the first tower that was hit and I met Gonzalves, a Mexican who loved Arizona, and who this year was cleaning windows in one of the two towers. He decided to keep me company for the next twenty minutes of my life, and I shared my shudder with him about what I saw. During our time together he told me that he did not know for sure what was happening but that something important was being "cooked", and he said cooking because great plans, very good or very bad, are not hatched, but cooked. I was surprised by his insight and began to think of several hypotheses.

Mr. Gonzalves always had the American dream and I told him that he would achieve it if he had faith and really believed in his possibilities. It is like the faith of ants when they dream of finding the perfect cheese. I admire people who believe in themselves, and Gonzalves was one of them. He had left his entire family in the magical city of Veracruz to seek a better working life in the United States, but that morning he was confused by his choice. Neither of us could imagine all that would happen that morning, the indescribable morning, as I have particularly defined it.

I am very fortunate to have been born in the city of Chicago. Both Mr. Parker and I, both from Chicago, embraced the friendly character of the city of Michigan years ago. For those of you who do not know and want to know about the character of the human being in the Windy City, I have always believed that the people of Chicago have a tax-free character and goodness. I will try to explain to myself, if the world were a dining room, the birds would come to the table where the people of Chicago are eating their lunch, because they have a special gift, they have the same respect for you whether you decide to be silent or whether you decide to talk. I suppose I love this city and its people madly.

Because of my friendly nature, I have always believed that I have been the perfect beggar to tell the most impressive story ever to have happened in America, the collapse of the two colossal and twin buildings.

Mr. Gonzalves used to tell me, in the funniest way possible, that the U.S. had usurped territory from Mexico. He would always tell me the battles over territoriality between these two countries, and I would always answer him the same thing when the tone of the conversation became a little sour, of course, without compromising friendship, "Really, Gonzalves, are you serious? I love the country that has better ramps to be able to slide my wheelchair, I have no problem giving up territory because I have always thought that the earth only belongs to God and the border issue is something too old-fashioned. There should be no borders, this is something doing a lot of harm to humanity. Paintings in a museum can cross borders and people can't do it! It's like letting a beautiful painting through and not letting the painter through. Ideas are allowed to pass through, but not people! I will always repeat this, the sooner we open the borders the sooner we will get used to the different ways of being of each other. It is key, people need the example as a form of education, and the frontiers prevent it, because constant eye contact is needed to learn, and technology does not come close. I want to meet people from other places without having to pay, it is denigrating for the human being. Borders are crossed by books, and people cannot do that. We have to reflect! Really Gonzalves, do you think that to go from one land to another or to cross from one desert to another you should have to ask for permission? It's something I could never understand.

If you want me to tell you the truth, my limits are the lack of ramps; it is such a tiny detail that goes unnoticed by the immensity of the people, Gonzalves, that I often start to cry alone, because I feel that the moonlight does not shine or reflect the same on the wheels of a chair as it does on some unpolluted shoes, like the ones you are wearing right now. That is my territoriality and those are my boundaries, seeing how human beings do not enjoy the reflection of moonlight on their shoes at nightfall. A lot of people who don't realize the enormous beam of light they have in their lives and decide to turn it off with their harmful conversations that only manage to annoy the neediest like me.

I still remember my teacher Gonzalves, dear Gonzalves, that person that society no longer values, but has the most important role. He told me that I would see great events in this world and that I should be an example for the future society.

Every day I see thousands of people crossing the streets, some with a smile on their lips, others very serious or talking on the phone and friends sleeping between cartons, but we all have a common background, we are all in love with life. That morning, New York suffered a forced disaffection from life, a forced absence of oxygen. Just because there are trees doesn't mean there's always oxygen.

I have always believed, my friend, that this society has a great problem: the great selfishness that exists. I detect a bipolarity not in behavior, but in intelligence focused on selfishness, a competition, as if we were ants looking for sweet gum or chewing gum from the ground.

Every day of my life, human beings have helped me in my daily work, but that day, 9/11, it was my turn to help; it is something that only life and its inexplicable nature can teach you. I am very sad that it took a day like this to fully develop all my potential for solidarity. I wish I had never been as supportive as I was on the 11th, because I would have preferred that the great setback of my life had never happened, that is, that those who need help would come to help.

Frankly, I believe that the most perfect plans and the evilest ones that one can come up with are carried out in the most silent way possible, with as few people as possible. When one hatches an evil plan, such as a terrorist attack of devastating proportions, one can devise it from one's home and with the fireplace lit. That day I told Gonzalves that there was very dense, very black smoke coming out of one of the towers, as if from a chimney, and then I said, "I want to ask you a question about evil planning, who is going to notice that black smoke coming out of a chimney in the wee hours of the morning? Here's a clue, in the secondary things of the different situations. You will probably notice from outside a house the light burning inside the room or the glare of computer light reflected off the white walls, but you will never pay attention to the smoke coming out of chimneys in homes or, in other words, the secondary things. It is that black smoke, only inhaled by the stars, which must really frighten us. It's like trying to detect the light of a candle on a star or trying to find out where the water jet from the whale is going to come out when they breathe; it is very difficult to know. Mexican friend, you have goodness in your blood, you love dialogue and jokes, I love that attitude, there are also a number of human beings in the world who are silent for prayer and that is great and wonderful, but there is another portion of beings who are embedded in that silence, where a person can relate it, unquestionably, with the black smoke that comes from the chimneys. It is not possible to capture the essence of their thoughts nor the root of the umbilical cord to their feelings, they are simply impenetrable. Okay, I agree with the utmost respect for those who love silence, but it's time to put a flashlight through the chimneys and see what's going on. Throughout my life... I have been praying and asking for peace in this world that is going to the edge of the cliff because of blind selfishness, and I need an overwhelming silence in my prayers, but not to plot a plan with God, but simply so that the smoke coming out of my chimney will reach the sky with no interest at all. It is a pure and un-strident prayer, which makes the night darker and the heartbeat of Lake Michigan brighter, is inexplicable.

"The problem with human prayer is when the prayers have a why and an explanation, that's what's really scary," Gonzalves answered me "look friend, I'm Mexican, although by my name many think I'm Portuguese or Brazilian, and I'm lucky enough to have seen the pure blue of the Pacific and to have prayed in front of it without intermittence and without hesitation, every human being should contemplate the blue of the Pacific to calm his soul; that's the inexplicable part of my life, you've told me yours and I've told you mine. You speak magic of the Michigan Lake and I of the Pacific, you praise a lake and I praise an ocean, and yet we get along so well you and I, a lake and an ocean can become great friends. Let me tell you something: at night all the boats are grazing on the sea, but only one of them is purely illuminated by the moonlight. There are human beings who, for whatever reason, are illuminated by who knows what, they will surely call it God, but what I am half clear about is that this world is unfair because the sun shines more for some than for others, and there is no way to alleviate this inequality, no matter what policies you make, it makes no sense to fight against the intense blue of the Pacific or against the selfishness of moonlight, it is irremediable. Politics should fight for an equal distribution of currencies and nothing else, because the other type of equality or inequality is already taken care of by nature". I continued with the conversation "hey Gonzalves, I heard another rumble, I don't know why. Well, my world revolves around ramps, I dream of having my own motorway so I can drive, but you are quite right, no policy can make it easier for me to move my wheelchair in a headwind or not skate when there is water and mud. I agree Gonzalves, I think this world should be less critical of the political class. I am more than ever an ant, Gonzalves, I am going too slowly today compared to any other human being. Let no one forget that for a disabled person it is three times as difficult to escape. I believe that the one who is in the first positions of intelligence is the one who begins to criticize the political class very little and simply dedicates himself to helping the needy people around him in silence. I have been a needy Gonzalves for many years, and I believe that divine providence has reserved a day for me when it will be my turn to help. It is incredible, but we all have a day saved in the calendar of our life in which our own contradiction appears in our own flesh. Experience is useless when there are situations from the past that make a parody of your personal life experience. It's as if the memories were laughing out loud at you in an uncontrolled way, without any modesty, and I think that's what's happening to me right now. I have the feeling, Gonzalves, that the black smoke coming out of the majestic towers is laughing out loud at me, now it's my turn to help people in need more than ever, in the next few days, inexplicably. During part of the morning of this sunny day, I got four and a half dollars, it is a triumph, solidarity of Mr. Parker or Miss Conrad apart. Normally I don't get to three dollars at this time of the morning, it is very clear that the passers-by go straight to work and forget about my particular condumio. The workers are automatons who go straight to please their own ego, without looking left or right. I do not know if it is right or wrong, but what it's clear to me is that those who go to work like robots, do not have God in their lives, because when you have the one who holds the clouds without columns in your life, there is a small pause on the way to any place. I will never understand people who do not make the pause, I am passionate about seeing some human beings who greet me from afar without stopping, is genuine, they pause without stopping, is magical because such people let glimpse something good, some fantastic vibrations transformed into the form of a greeting. What can I say? for me a greeting is something very valuable because it reminds me that among human beings, we should shake hands, even though physically sometimes it doesn't happen, I don't care if it is from a distance. By the way, Gonzalves, I have never told you this and it is about time I told you, you are a great listener and I would like to give you my last opinion before going to visit Walter Ryscott, because last Thursday I told him that I would go to his house to have a cup of tea, there are silences that can be scary, like some statues that seem to be looking at you continuously, although I agree with what you once told me, Gonzalves, that the statues also tremble. They also give themselves away in some way or another, which happens to be almost impossible to detect, it's like trying to locate an ant in the tar.

Within the great variety of human beings that exist in what remains of the planet, there are different types of generations, the generation of peace, where the birds embrace the clouds; the volcanic generation, which is full of anger and waits for the exact moment to explode; the cryptic generation, which is practically indecipherable in its thoughts, that is, you know the starch but not its chemical formula ($C_6H_{10}O_5$); and the best, or worst of all generations if mixed with some of the previous ones, the silent generation, the smoke from the chimney in the middle of the night, which is only seen by the stars and which only, my friend, God detects. Not always is fire worse than smoke, sometimes smoke heralds something even more devastating. It is he, God, who sees the ant in the tar. Come on Gonzalves, don't give me those references of yours that the silent generation is of this or that origin, I'm going to go back to listening to your obsolete argument, you and I know, the Pacific and the Michigan, that there is a type of people who camouflage themselves in the very human noise, who go into the universe of silence, where most human beings cannot reach.

Finally, I said goodbye saying "hey, I'm going to Walter Ryscott's house to see what's up with him, tomorrow I hope to see you again if those two towers don't fall apart. Give me a cigarette, I've given my lungs enough of a holiday, I feel like giving a good puff to one of yours".

I like talking to people in the street, it's something I've always done, I don't know if it's a mania or not, the truth is that I do it almost without stopping.

I arrived at Walter Ryscott's house, I asked him how he was, and I told him that I was fine, although with a little more gray hair on my head and legs, he began to talk to me, "here I am, watching television, very attentive to what is happening minutes away, in fact my wife appeared on television walking near the north tower, I could see that she was bringing the bag of fruit that I asked her to bring from the supermarket. I think it was two planes that crashed into the towers, and everything points to it being a terrorist attack. The President will soon say a few words.

I answered my host, "Dear Walter Ryscott, you know something, birds and airplanes have and always will have the shape of a crucifix, I know you are a Christian and as a Christian I have the feeling that you have never stopped to think about this, birds, those unique birds, have that great gift of being able to fly, I have always believed them to be the true angels of the earth because they are the only beings that can walk in the sky without the need of any machinery; look at the wonderful landing of the storks in their nests. Everything that is artificial... spoils in some way or another the flight towards the blue of the sky. Walter Ryscott, it does seem overwhelming, the impact of the planes on the towers. Oh, my God, now there's a lot of smoke coming out of that side of the North Tower.

I asked him to please put one more spoonful of sugar in my coffee, that sugar that ants love, my friend Walter Ryscott continued with the conversation "why do we hurt each other so much", I listen to him carefully while I take a few sips of the coffee. Once he finished speaking, I answered him "I think that in this world there are talkative people and silent people, that is the real division of human beings, when the parameters of one and the other are triggered, conflict appears. Extreme silence and endless talking are what makes wars appear, and they are practically inevitable because the middle ground between the two is almost unreachable and impossible". My friend asked me, "How would you get someone who is extremely silent to join the wheel of dialogue? I know this is very difficult to answer, but an approximated idea would suffice. I said "Look, the person who is used to silence is very comfortable at the bottom of his ocean. This is the typical person who doesn't mind the passage of time, because, for them, the passage of time is like the swell of the sea, after one wave another will come and that's it, there's nothing more to tell; But if we have to point out something very important about it, is that the silent person can't stand the tsunami of words from the talker, the talker may feel a little uncomfortable with the silent person, but the silent person is the one who, deep down, rumbles the most about their actions. They are like the great basketball player who feels that he is the best while he chews gum, he knows clearly that any ball he catches, he scores, so he doesn't care what anyone says or doesn't say about him. The silent person is the same, they know that they always have an ace up their sleeve, a secret they will never tell anyone, and so they simply listens to others, paying a little attention but not giving it too much importance, as if what you are going to tell them, they'd already heard too many times or seen it... in another life. People who fall within the genre of silence are extraordinary human beings, with an intelligence out of the ordinary, they are people who can approach a quasi-divine morality and that, oddly enough, is what this world lacks, a lot of morality to be able to face the future. They have the quality of being kind to the people around them, but, as I told you before, I do not know to what extent they put up with the other extreme, the talker. Walter Ryscott said to me, "I've always liked your chats, where can we find that kind of person? I mean the quiet ones, because I'm quite a chatterbox. I answered him "the first thing you have to do to detect that type of person is to try to get as close as possible to silence, which must be an effort for you because you are not used to it. Imagine that you don't know how to speak the language, you can hardly relate to anyone, you would pass at once to that silent type, although it doesn't consist exactly in that or in elevator conversations... Well, I think we'll leave that talk for next time because the first tower is falling down. We watched in exaltation the images on the television "oh my God, for heaven's sake, who would have been able to carry out that atrocity?, I think the one who did it, dear Walter Ryscott, must have been out of the ordinary cold-blooded, don't you think?" to which he said "Yes, I think it's too much. I went on to say, "Let's wait and see, my chair has shaken under my belt. Walter Ryscott said, "Do you want me to tell you something? I don't believe that future prophets stand behind a computer screen. Do you really believe that the one who has to come and save us stands behind a computer screen?" I answered "I definitely believe, Walter Ryscott, that there are many teachers on the face of the earth and few prophets. There is a big difference. People who resemble the prophets are stripped, as in antiquity, of everything that is heavy. They are walking the streets, walking their eyes to one side or the other without paying much attention to the course of events, they are not seers, but they do predict or warn about what will happen. He said "I have to ask you a question. You know there are a number of people who are dedicated to carry out their day to day trying to have the least possible contact with everything and anything that resembles the human being; how will these people, who choose to give their lives to non-human contact without harming anyone... can be judged by God? God has no content to be able to evaluate them, can silence really be evaluated or qualified?," to which I answered "I respect people who bet on silence, but, my God, I hope they bet on the symbols of peace, because otherwise the future is not very hopeful. Those extremely intelligent people who make it so difficult for God, but who, at the same time, do not offend Him or give the Almighty the shaft. It is very difficult to answer that, because qualifying the silence of people is the most difficult task God has, the easy thing is to put a grade on the common, what we see in everyday life, to see if a person greets you or turns their back on you, if they try to swindle you or if they insult you because of the color of your skin, yet it is impossible, or I do not know how to do it, that which is only seen by the eyes of silence. It's like the silent trust, the trust of a human in a volcano or the trust of an ant in the sole of a shoe, it's too strange. Once... I heard that God sends earthquakes to places where there is too much noise, because he wants silence for humans to practice prayer, I think it must be very difficult", Walter Ryscott answered me: "you and I believe in God, I still struggle to find an answer and there is no way, man, it is a code with too many hidden ciphers. Of the immensity of options, the game of chess gives you, there's one that nobody would bet on, not even a machine or a computer, and that's where the generation of silence is, where almost nobody can go".

I changed the subject to "I'd like to say hello to your wife, Mara. You were in Honduras not long ago, how is your family, Walter Ryscott?" he replied, "very well, although her parents are already getting very old and that is something that cannot be stopped, my friend; we want to return by next June. There's still a long way to go, but well, we'll take one of those flying crucifixes, as you call them, and we'll go back to Honduran lands. I love that country, and I like countries that try to go as unnoticed as possible, like Honduras, where the people are very humble; that's priceless.

"I like that too, Walter Ryscott, even though there isn't a city, or even a country, in the world that can compete with Chicago. I've walked around this city and I've come to a strong conclusion: Chicago is one thing and America is another. There's a big difference, dear Walter Ryscott, don't laugh, man! I admit, when I talk about Chicago, I get excited, I can't help it, dude. The only city that has seen me without a wheelchair has been the city of wind. I have cried too much, I will repeat it a thousand times, it is the city where everything and nothing happens at the same time. It is like a restless mystery that wants to be revealed and at the same time decides, at the last minute, to keep its secret. Having said all this, my friend Walter Ryscott, what I do recognize is that on September 11th, I stopped walking, I will never forget that day. Something tears my soul apart when I see so many people complaining about everything, everything bothers them. I remember that fateful 9/11 quite a few years ago, the moment when everything was going to change in my life forever. People who are healthy must skip and hop through the streets; must enter the cafes with a smile from ear to ear; must pat their father on the back when he enters the door of their house and must laugh a lot when they argue with someone at the end of the conversation; that's life, appreciate what health has to offer. The moment you don't appreciate your raw breath, as far as health is concerned, you are throwing something away and it will be irretrievable, let there be no doubt about that. I have always believed in one thing, there are people who feel a tremendous lack of motivation for life, it's as if nothing catches their interest. I think they are a group of individuals with a set of neurons superior to the rest of the mortals. Note that possessing superior neurons or infinite intelligence is not the equivalent to be a better person. How is it possible that there are people on this planet in which their greatest aspiration is to talk or to meet face to face with God to chat? This is something, Walter Ryscott, that surpasses my understanding". And I continued: "Listen, I have the possibility to have a house, buy a car or completely ignore my beautiful and excited wife's dreams, but I don't feel like it, what I want is simply to be left in peace once and for all and to achieve my goal or objective, which is none other than what God "supposedly" wants. I don't give a damn if my wife is excited about her pregnancy, I do not care at all if they have raised the price of water or whatever, what is really important to me is not found in this or any other planet. No one should forget that peace between two diametrically opposed societies is impossible, no one will find a solution to it, and this is not a disease that can be cured by treatment, no sir, not even a terminal disease which can be saved by a miracle. This goes much further and, for the first time, the figure of God appears clearly in this shamble and in which he feels sincerely uncomfortable. There are people who are extremely intelligent but who lack the real morality to be able to face this colossal problem, and for all that, with the current paradigm, we are going to have a horrifying clash of civilizations. This model will break, sooner or later, like the thread of a kite. The world needs us to intermingle from a very young age if we are to avoid a clash between humans. What you do while talking... someone else does the same thing but in silence, an insurmountable difference, but there is hope for the future if this mingling takes place as soon as possible.

Currently, there are beings embedded within society who do not want to know anything about it. It is possible to be perfectly imbued with society and have no mercy on it; they really become beings guided by an annoying selfishness, but clearly accepted; only when difficult times come, does the fearful anger jump out at them. The disappearance of the pause in conversation, or of contemplation, is turning this society into a relentlessly hyperactive engine which, in the end, ends up making everyone angry and inevitably, leads to war. I ask myself a question: what is more dangerous, the silence of money or the noise of a missile? Fear really produces silence and noise at the same time... and halfway through, there is war. People do not reflect on children dying of hunger while different societies smile freely and unrestrainedly. Future governments must fight against counter-technology. I'll explain myself friends. As an example, we must pay attention to the sale of knives and forks, there is no point in having tanks available as they are not as valuable anymore, those mastodontic armatures, in order to safeguard life".

When the terrorist goes to the hairdresser's, he doesn't usually say how he wants his hair cut. He lets them cut it in their own way and thus, gets to know his rival. Terrorism has a great ally, bureaucracy, the great geniuses of good or evil, despise bureaucracy. The killer bees immolate themselves to defend their hive while the terrorists do not know their real reason, but we should be very attentive. Let us not forget that even without a warrant for war, a country can also be perfectly destabilized. America does not need equilibristat (on railways, device to measure the deviation of the balance of a wagon when driving in a curve), it is the only continent that allows you to have nightmares at night, to dream at dawn, and for your dreams to come true. America is grand because of its small gestures. I cannot get out of my head that woman who was in a wheelchair, like me, trying as she could to clean the excrement her dog had just deposited on the sidewalk of a remote and lost street in Chicago.

The United States is a country that has something no other country has. Those stripes on its flag show it, made and placed consciously by destiny so the old railroads of the beautiful city of New York continue to circulate; that lack of doubt and roar towards the future with some passengers guided by the stars which illuminate their flag, their paths and their citizens. Los Angeles, and precisely from Los Angeles to New York, passing, of course, through Chicago, in order to protect the color and brilliance of the American flag. May God, always, bless America.

www.ingramcontent.com/pod-product-compliance
Lightning Source LLC
LaVergne TN
LVHW041541060526
838200LV00037B/1086